Secrets of Success

By Chris Quigley

Introduction

What is success?

Success isn't just about money.
It is about happiness, choices
and feeling good about yourself.
Successful people feel good about:

- How hard they have tried.
- Who they are.
- What they spend their time doing.
- The choices they have in their lives.

Here are some things everyone should know...

- You are not born successful.
- Everyone has setbacks and failures.
- The first step to success is choosing.

DO YOU WANT TO BE SUCCESSFUL?

EVERYONE can be successful by following the eight secrets in this book.

Secrets of Success

Published by Chris Quigley Education Limited

First published April 2010

ISBN 978-0-9559095-6-6

Acknowledgements

This book is inspired by the work of Richard St. John and Sir Ken Robinson.

Thanks to 2B Graphics Ltd for design and print production.

This book is for my parents, Pat and Tony who pushed me. Thank you!

Don't give up

Try new things

Work hard

Understand others

SECRET SUCCESS SECRET

Concentrate

Improve

Imagine

Push yourself

Contents

Try new things

Find something to be good at

The first step to success is finding something to be good at.
Successful people are always trying new things.
How many things have you tried this week?

Find your ENERGY ZONE

Successful people love what they are doing.
They have found their E Zone.
You know when you are there...

SECRET SUCCESS SECRET

- When work feels like play.
- When time flies by.
- When you just don't want to stop.
- When you just don't notice anything else.

If you don't try lots of new things you might never find your ENERGY ZONE.

So... keep trying new things.

Finding your E Zone CHANGES EVERYTHING

You can try lots of things and enjoy them but when you really love something... **YOU GET ENERGY.**

Things that stop you finding your E Zone

- Not trying out new things.
- Pressure from your friends who might think it is not cool to try some things.

Finding your CREW

Your crew is other people who love doing the same things as you. You might find them by trying out:

clubs or groups

When you find your crew you feel

- Valued, because you find other people **JUST LIKE YOU.**
- Challenged, because sometimes they help to **PUSH YOU.**

Try new things

Life is not a STRAIGHT LINE

You might feel that you know what you want to do when you are older. That's fine but what if it doesn't turn out to be something you love doing?

By trying lots of things you might fall into something you love doing.

Most people don't know what they want to do when they are older, so keep trying new things and you might find something you love.

REMEMBER

Trying new things is an important way to become successful but some things may cost a lot of money.

These things may need to wait until you have saved up or until you are older and can pay for them yourself.

But... many things don't cost anything like trying new ways to do things or taking the chance to do things at school.

SECRET SUCCESS SECRET

HERE ARE THE RULES

Successful people

- [x] Try lots of new things.
- [x] Find their E Zone.
- [x] Enjoy having a go.
- [x] Look out for opportunities.

Unsuccessful people

- ✗ Don't have a go.
- ✗ Don't enjoy what they do.
- ✗ Don't see opportunities.
- ✗ Don't try new things.

Make a list of new things you could try.

2 Work hard

NO SHORT CUTS

If you want to get really good at something there are **no short cuts – it's all about practising**. Now that's not something everyone wants to hear but it's true.

Just think about anyone who is really good at something and ask him or her how he or she became good at it.

If you are finding something tricky to understand, working at it really helps.

WORK IS GOOD

Some people think that work is something that we should avoid. These people are not successful! Successful people don't make fun of work because they know it leads to success. They have a good attitude to work. In fact, successful people have fun working. This is because it challenges them and better still they can see it working.

If you ask anyone really successful why they are working so hard, they usually say "because I enjoy it!" Working can be fun but that doesn't mean laughing all the time, just getting on and working hard can be fun.

Put in the hours

Working hard isn't just for a short time. It can take hours and hours. The more time you spend working at something, the better. Don't be in too much of a hurry to become really good at something. It can take a long time.

There is no 'over night' success, just hours and hours of hard work.

What do you think of the following saying?

The difference between try and triumph is a little umph.

It means that to get great at something – to triumph, you need to try AND work hard. **(Umph is the noise of someone working hard!)**

It's not easy

Working hard isn't easy

Some people make things look easy but they have worked hard in order to become good at what they are doing.

So when you see successful people don't ever think they are different from you. Don't ever think that it was easy for them – it wasn't. They worked hard, had fun, put the hours in and sometimes had to really push themselves – **HARD!**

SECRET SUCCESS SECRET

This is one of the biggest secrets of this handbook.

SUCCESS IS NOT EASY FOR ANYONE

Work hard

Time to think

Think about someone successful. Write down the things they might have had to work at to become a success.

What do you find hard? Write down one or two things you find really hard and make a promise to yourself to practise more.

Find someone to push you... so you don't avoid doing things that are hard.

Hang around with people who like to work hard. This will inspire you to work hard too.

Work AND Play

Some people separate their lives into parts

- **Going go work (or school).**
- **Having fun.**

But successful people don't do this. They have fun working and work hard at things that are fun.

HERE ARE THE RULES

Successful people

- ☑ Practise lots.
- ☑ Know that this works.
- ☑ Enjoy working hard.
- ☑ Put in the hours.

Unsuccessful people

- ☒ Don't practise.
- ☒ Make fun of hard workers.
- ☒ Enjoy sitting around.
- ☒ Don't do the work.

Which things do you need to do more of to work hard?

Some things can stop you concentrating

To get good at anything, you need to concentrate and get it done but that's not always as easy as it sounds. Things can stop you from concentrating like...

- TV.
- Games consoles.
- Browsing the Internet.
- Trying to do too many things at once.
- Friends.

Avoid distractions

When you have something important to do, keep way from distractions. Don't switch on the TV or anything that might look more fun than what you are doing. When you have homework to do find a quiet place and concentrate.

LEARN TO 'TUNE OUT' DISTRACTIONS

If you can't avoid distractions you can learn to tune out the things that put you of

This is useful in noisy classrooms or if someone near to you is being a distraction.

This one takes practice and is much easier when you are really clear about what you are doing.

Be clear about what you are doing

Once you are really clear about what you are doing, it is easier to concentrate.

Some people like to:

- Draw pictures to help them understand what they are doing.
- Talk through what they are doing with others.
- Break things down into steps so that they don't get distracted.

What helps you to concentrate?

Become an expert

As you try lots of things you will hopefully find some that you love doing. These are the things that you might find yourself doing more often. In other words, you are concentrating.

If you really concentrate, you can become an expert. To be really successful, you need to be an expert at something. If you are really good at something then you are an expert.

Do the right things

Concentrating isn't just about getting on with something and doing it well. It is also about doing the right things well. In other words, you need to know which things are important. If a designer was asked to make a leather handbag but instead concentrated on some shoes, it doesn't really matter how good the shoes are – there's no bag!

Some people call this prioritising **– which means putting things in order of how important they are. Start with the most important things then move on to less important things.**

Concentrate

HERE ARE THE RULES

Successful people

- ☑ Concentrate.
- ☑ Tune out distractions.
- ☑ Focus on the right things.
- ☑ Learn what helps them concentrate.

Unsuccessful people

- ☒ Don't concentrate.
- ☒ Are easily distracted.
- ☒ Don't focus.
- ☒ Don't know what helps them concentrate.

Which things do you need to do more of to concentrate?

4 Push yourself

Push yourself in lots of ways

To be really successful you need to push yourself...

- When you don't feel like doing things.
- When you don't think you'll be good enough.
- When you feel shy.
- When your friends try to stop you from doing what you want to do.

It can be difficult to push yourself but it really does help you to become successful.

How to push yourself:

Choose something you want to do or achieve. This is called a goal. Some people call them targets. Goals can be anything you like. **They can be big goals or small ones... you decide.**

Here are some examples of goals:

- I want to be able to play drums.
- I want to learn disco dancing.
- I want to learn the 7 times table.
- I want to climb Mount Everest.

When you have a goal you start to do things that help you reach your goal. Goals work best when they are things you really want to do, but seem hard – **that's why you need to push yourself to do them.**

4 Push yourself

Deadlines

A deadline is a time by when you need to do something. "I need to get this homework finished by Friday, so I can sleep over at my friends house at the weekend."

If something is difficult to do, setting a deadline helps to stop you putting it off.

If your parents want you to do something that you don't feel like doing, ask for a deadline and then you can build up towards doing it.

Fight your fears

Sometimes we get scared.

Sometimes we know we are scared and other times we don't realise it but just don't feel right.

Either way it can stop us from doing things. It can stop us from joining in because we might be shy. It can stop us trying new things because we are not sure what it will be like. Our brains are very good at talking us out of things that make us feel scared or uncomfortable. This keeps us in our comfort zone and away from our E Zone.

A comfort zone sounds pretty good but the problem is, we never try out new things if we don't push ourselves, so...we need to be FEAR FIGHTERS.

HOW TO BE A 'FEAR FIGHTER'

Write down the things that make you feel uncomfortable. **Here are some examples:**

- Talking to new people.
- Going to new places where you don't know anybody.
- Answering questions in front of the class.
- Asking questions in front of others.
- Having a go at solving problems.

SECRET SUCCESS SECRET

These are just some of the fears we might have. Once you have written your list, try to do something small every day to fight your fears.

We all like to hear "well done" – but sometimes we need to say it to ourselves.

If you find it hard to push yourself, give yourself a treat if you manage to push past things that are stopping you. If your challenge is to speak to a new person or go somewhere new, **treat yourself to something you really like,** once you have done it.

4 Push yourself

Ask for help

It is not easy to keep finding the energy to push yourself. Sometimes we need help. Find someone you trust to keep reminding you about goals, deadlines and fighting your fears. **It might be a friend, family member or teacher... maybe all of them!**

Don't be afraid to tell people you are struggling – it happens to

EVERY SINGLE PERSON IN THE WORLD

Even people who make things look easy!

-Sports coaches, music, dance or drama teachers -chess champions or anyone who is an **EXPERT** might be good **MENTOR**. A mentor is someone who can coach and guide you – **someone you trust to give you good advice and guidance.**

LISTEN TO PEOPLE WHO CARE

It may seem like a lecture or even like a telling-off but people who care for you **WANT YOU TO DO WELL.** It might not feel like it when they are nagging you to practise piano or learn your times tables or do your homework. They are pushing you because they can see that you might be finding it hard to push yourself.

Teachers, family – even annoying brothers or sisters, friends and anyone else who cares about you will always be pushing you. Try to listen to them...

Remember, they CARE about you and WANT you to SUCCEED.

HERE ARE THE RULES

Successful people

- ☑ Push themselves.
- ☑ Fight their fears.
- ☑ Ask for help.
- ☑ Listen to others who care.

Unsuccessful people

- ☒ Don't push themselves.
- ☒ Let their fears stop them.
- ☒ Don't ask for help.
- ☒ Don't listen to others who care.

Which things do you need to do more of to push yourself?

Imagine what things could be like?

Successful people imagine what things could be like – even if things aren't very good now. If you want things to change, first you have to think about how they could be. This is creative thinking.

Have ideas

The only way to be really creative is to have ideas. That sounds like it may be a bit tricky but here's the good bit...

they don't always have to be good ideas.

Most good ideas only come after lots of bad ideas. Try to have lots of ideas every day and then work out which are good and which are not so good. Give yourself an award for having lots of bad ideas, as long as they don't do anyone any harm.

REMEMBER: GREAT IDEAS ONLY COME FROM PEOPLE WHO ARE WILLING TO BE WRONG!

SECRET SUCCESS SECRET

MY LIST OF BAD IDEAS:

Invest in a MAGIC WAND... I mean a PEN.
Always write down your ideas otherwise they will disappear. Have an ideas book so you can look back at all of your good and bad ideas.

LISTEN TO OTHER PEOPLE

- Use your **ears for ideas.**
- Listening gives you the chance to see what other people might want. This might give you an idea.

Steal ideas!

Take but don't be a fake!

Steal ideas... and make them better.

Look around and see what others are doing and take their ideas. Its OK to take other people's ideas but you can't pretend they are your own until you make them better.

Ask questions

How many good questions did you ask today?

The only foolish questions are the ones you don't ask.

Don't always expect your teachers or parents to know the answers... it might be your job to find out the answers and tell them.

Imagine

WHEN TO ASK QUESTIONS

If you are in the classroom, you might ask questions about something you are doing. If you are outdoors, you might ask questions about what you can see. In fact... **you can ask questions anywhere and at any time.**

Sometimes it might be best to save your questions for another time... **like when the teacher is talking or in the middle of a telling off from your parents.**

But...DID YOU KNOW?

Most questions we ask are

When you look at a clock you are silently asking **"What time is it?"**

When you turn over the pages of a book you might be asking
" I wonder how many pages left?"

When you try out an idea you are usually asking a question.
" I wonder what will happen if...?"

SECRET SUCCESS SECRET

So... if you find it hard to ask your questions out loud, don't worry.

Try out lots of ideas and you'll be asking lots of questions.

Be creative

Creativity is all about using your imagination to come up with something **USEFUL.**

CREATIVITY IS ALL ABOUT USEFUL IDEAS

You might come up with lots of ideas but the next trick is to try to make sure your ideas give something useful to the world.

Look at the examples:

Idea	Use
Building a swimming pool in the desert.	No people to use it. (Not much use)
Building a swimming pool on spare land near the school.	Lots of people to use it. (Lots of use)
Inventing a flying tin opener that sings.	Flies too high to catch it when you want some beans on toast, so you can't open the tin of beans. (Not much use)

5 Imagine

Useful ideas

How do you know if an idea is useful? **Here are a few ways:**

- Does it solve a problem?
- Does it help someone?
- Is it fun?
- Would people enjoy it?
- Does it help you to understand something better?
- Would people find it interesting?
- Does it give information?

WRITE SOME USEFUL IDEAS

IDEA	USE

Happy mistakes

Sometimes, you might have an idea that you think might be useful in one way, but it turns out to have a different use... **even better than the one you thought of.**

These are called HAPPY MISTAKES.

The best things invented by mistake:

Anti-biotics: Alexander Fleming didn't clean up his workstation before going on holiday one day. When he came back, he noticed that there was a strange fungus on some of his mixtures. Even stranger there were no germs on or near the mixtures. He had discovered something that would kill bacteria. **Thousands of lives have been saved by this mistake!**

Coca Cola: John Pemberton was trying to make a cure for headaches. He mixed together a bunch of ingredients (which they keep secret!) and ended up with a fizzy drink instead.

It is a good job that these people made mistakes!

5 Imagine

BRING YOUR IDEAS TO LIFE

Once you have useful ideas, you need to get them out of your head and into real life. **Successful people are creative people who DO THINGS.**

You could have a great idea to write a story about a talking dog that saves the world from an evil cat. It is a useful idea because people would enjoy reading it. But what if you don't get round to writing it and it stays in your head?

CREATIVE PEOPLE THINK LOTS AND DO LOTS.

How could you bring ideas to life?

- Writing things down?
- Making things?
- Drawing?
- Filming?

Amazing brain fact No.1

Your brain acts out your imagination.

Try the paper clip trick.

Instructions:

YOU WILL NEED: A paper clip or a small weight; thread or string.

- Tie the paper clip to a thread.
- Hold it out in front of you, keeping your arm straight.
- Look at the paper clip and really imagine it going round and round in a circle.

You'll be amazed! The paper clip starts to move... all by itself!

This is because your brain loves to be right... so if you can imagine something strong enough it finds ways to make things happen.

Amazing brain fact No.2

Your brain looks out for things that interest you.

It notices things that are interesting to you. It sometimes notices things even when you are not thinking about them! That's when **AN IDEA JUST POPS INTO YOUR HEAD.**

The more you think about your useful ideas and the more you imagine them happening, your brain will help you to come up with a way!

AMAZING BRAIN FACT NO.3

Your brain believes what you tell it most of the time.

If you tell yourself that you **CAN** do things, your brain will believe you.
If you tell yourself that you **CAN'T** do things, your brain will believe you.

SECRET SUCCESS SECRET

So You need to THINK CLEVER.

Never, ever think that you are not clever. Your brain might believe it and then it will come up with ways to make it true!

HERE ARE THE RULES

Successful people

- ☑ Have ideas (sometimes bad ones!)
- ☑ Use their imagination.
- ☑ Think lots and DO lots.
- ☑ Believe they can have ideas.

Unsuccessful people

- ☒ Don't have enough ideas.
- ☒ Don't imagine much.
- ☒ Don't act on their ideas.
- ☒ Don't believe they can have ideas.

Which things do you need to do more of to imagine?

6 Improve

Small steps

Successful people are always trying to make things better. That doesn't mean there is anything wrong with what they have but... **they imagine the possibilities.**

They imagine what things could be like if they were just a bit better. They make lots of small improvements rather than big changes. Some people call this tweaking or refining. Successful people are always looking for ways to make good things **GREAT!**

Great things don't happen suddenly – they come from lots and lots of tweaking and refining of good things. This is good news because it makes it much easier to be successful if we know **we can take small steps to greatness.**

JUST ONE THING

- If you have written a story, think of just one thing that would give more value to someone reading it.
- If you have made a new dance, think of just one thing that would make it more exciting to other people.
- If you are mastering a game, think of just one thing that might help to get you to the next level.

In fact, some people see small steps as the best way of getting to the next level. Instead of getting frustrated, take small steps to make things better.

Just a bit

You don't need to transform things to make them better – **just make small changes.** Think of just one thing to make just a little bit better.

Great things come from lots of small changes.

SECRET SUCCESS SECRET

DO YOUR BEST

Each time you have an idea or do some work... **do your best.**

Ask yourself, "Is this my very best ?" If it is, then it will probably be better then the last time you did it. If it's the first time you have done something, still aim to do your best and then next time try to do it even better.

Did you do your best today?

Don't be satisfied with just OK. Make good the starting point.

Improve

To hurry generally means getting things done as quickly as possible.

The trouble with hurrying is that it can lead to mistakes. When we make mistakes, the quality isn't as good as it could be... **so take your time and think about the quality of your work.**

SUCCESSFUL PEOPLE DON'T RUSH THEY CONCENTRATE ON QUALITY

NEVER STOP IMPROVING

Even when someone is really good at something, they can be just a little bit better.

Successful people are always trying to improve.

They never stop. In fact, one of the best ways to stop being successful is to stop improving.

That's why computers always seem out of date... because the computer companies keep trying to make them even better.

HERE ARE THE RULES

Successful people

- ☑ Take small steps.
- ☑ Make things just a bit better.
- ☑ Do their best.
- ☑ Don't rush.

Unsuccessful people

- ☒ Want success NOW.
- ☒ Don't improve.
- ☒ Don't give their best.
- ☒ Rush and make mistakes.

Which things do you need to do more of to improve?

Understand others

Being useful to others

Successful people don't just think about themselves. They often think about others. They want to do things that are **USEFUL** for other people.

Instead of asking "What can I get out of this?"

try asking "What can I give?"

If you find yourself in your E ZONE writing stories, that's fine, but to be a successful writer you need to write stories that other people enjoy reading.

If you find yourself in your E ZONE talking to other people, that's fine but if you want to become successful at presentations you need to present things that **other people want to hear**.

This is a really useful secret for anyone who owns a business: if you are selling something **other people want** – then you will be successful.

If you are selling things that **you want** then you might not be successful. Remember when we talked about creativity? We called it useful ideas. That's what understanding others is all about... giving other people something they find useful.

Here are some ways to try to understand others

If you really want to understand others ask them.

Ask them what they think of your plans.

They might give you some good ideas to think about.

Listen to feedback (teachers call this marking.) It is a great way of understanding what others think about your work or ideas. **Good feedback tells you what you are good at, where it could be better and** how to give more value to others. If you act on this feedback you are showing that you want to understand others.

SECRET SUCCESS SECRET

Understand others

Be careful what you listen to!

Some people don't give good feedback! You need to learn which feedback is useful and which is just critical. Look at these statements: which do you think are useful and which are just critical?

I like the way you started your dance but you need to move in time with the rest of the group.

- ☐ useful
- ☐ critical

Your science experiment was well thought out but you forgot to write down what you found out.

- ☐ useful
- ☐ critical

Your work is messy.

- ☐ useful
- ☐ critical

The first two examples are useful.

The last one isn't useful feedback. It just criticises. It's OK to ignore criticism but we should listen carefully to feedback.

This is where you look at your own pieces of work or ideas and try to see them as others would view them. To do this...

- Pick out the best bits and say why they are good.
- Think of ways your work could be even better.

People who reflect are usually very successful because they know they won't always have a teacher around to give feedback so... **they do it themselves!**

SEE BOTH SIDES

First, write down all of the good things about your ideas.

Then try to find faults.

Finally ask for help to put your faults right.

7 Understand others

Instead of thinking of good things about your work and ideas, **try to think about faults.** This sounds a bit negative, but **it is a good way** to find problems before anyone else does.

Businesses do this. Before Apple release a new iPod they try to find all the faults or bugs before the customers do. Then they put them right! They need to behave like customers to **understand them.** If you want to be a successful artist, try to find the faults in your own work before other people do. This will help you to make sure you always understand others. **Successful people** understand others whilst unsuccessful people think about themselves. To understand others you might need to **push yourself.** This is because when you put a lot of effort into something it is hard to change it or make it better.

It might be hard so we need to push ourselves.

Successful people

- ☑ Think about others.
- ☑ Listen to the views of others.
- ☑ Reflect.
- ☑ Find faults in their own work.

Unsuccessful people

- ☒ Think about themselves.
- ☒ Don't care what others think.
- ☒ Don't reflect.
- ☒ Let others find the faults in their work.

Which things do you need to do more of to understand others?

8 Don't give up

Keep going

In all of the chapters of this handbook we have talked about ways to be successful. All of the ways are important and it's hard to pick just one as the most important but the final secret is that...

successful people don't give up.

SECRET SUCCESS SECRET

Did you **know...**

Successful people have...

- bad luck
- setbacks
- failures
- criticism
- rejection

and they sometimes lose their energy to keep going but they **find a way around these problems.**

STICKABILITY

Some people call this resilience.

It means sticking with something:

- Even if something is distracting you.
- Even if something is really hard to do.
- Even if you fail first time.
- No matter what.

This is about dealing with failure, rejection or criticism.

Successful people do get upset when they fail but...

they dust themselves down and bounce back!

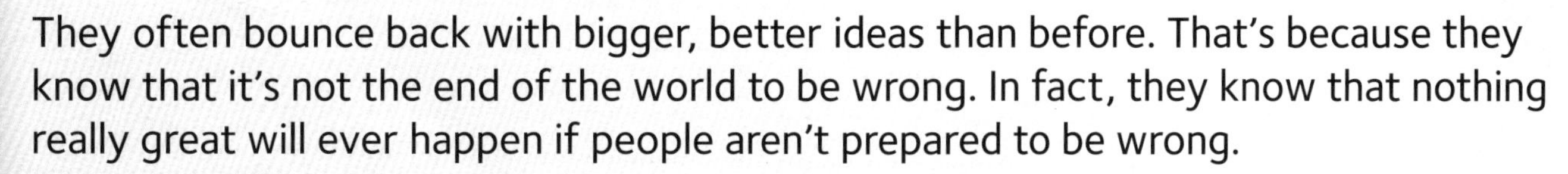
They often bounce back with bigger, better ideas than before. That's because they know that it's not the end of the world to be wrong. In fact, they know that nothing really great will ever happen if people aren't prepared to be wrong.

Can you think of times when you have had to bounce back? Can you remember how you felt when you failed and how much better you felt when you bounced back?

Sometimes you might want to do something but you don't have the money to do it. You could give up or you could bounce back with an idea.

Bouncing back gives you energy. Successful people are BOUNCY people.

8 Don’t give up

Learn from mistakes

Here’s another secret. Successful people make lots of mistakes but they usually don’t make the same mistake more than once. That’s because they learn from their mistakes. Learning from mistakes means thinking about next time.

When you make a mistake try not to be mean to yourself.

THINGS NOT TO SAY OR THINK.

- I’m always doing that!
- I can’t do it!
- I’m stupid!
- I’ll never be able to do it!

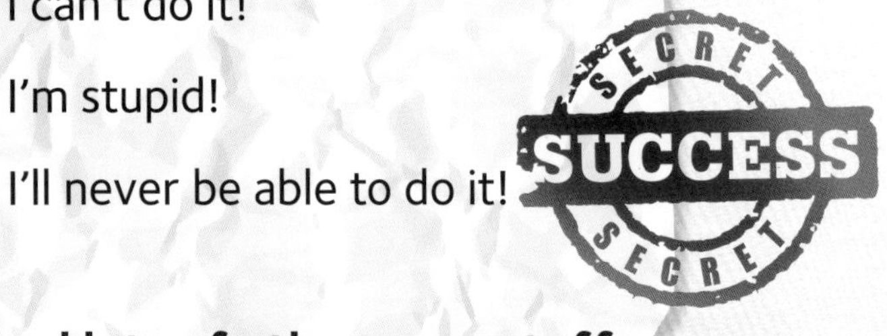

...and lots of other mean stuff.

It’s important not to because your brain might just believe you and it will come up with an easy solution... **QUIT.**

NEXT TIME

Successful people don't quit, so don't be mean to yourself. **Instead try:**

- I didn't think it though this time – **NEXT TIME** I will think carefully.
- I didn't work hard this time - **NEXT TIME** I will make sure I work harder.
- I didn't get the part in the school play because I didn't learn the lines properly. **NEXT TIME** I'll spend more time learning the lines.

Remember... If you don't give up there'll always be a next time but if you give up... **there may never be a next time.**

Talk to yourself

Some people call this self-talk.

This is the conversation you have with yourself in your head.

Here's the rules:

- Keep your self talk positive.
- Tell yourself that you can go on and finish what you started.
- Tell yourself that you are going to succeed and that you do have the ability.

8 Don't give up

Don't listen to criticism

Remember in the chapter on pushing yourself we talked about the difference between feedback and criticism?

The rule is listen to feedback and ignore criticism. Feedback is useful but criticism isn't.

SO IGNORE IT!

This is how lots of successful people keep going even when things get tough. If you are finding something really hard to do, try visualising yourself doing it. Make the images strong. Notice how good you feel. Try it now... **It really does work.**

Visualise

Here's the trick:

- Dream about how things will be if you keep going.
- Make the image strong and bright.
- Notice how good it feels.

Remember don't forget the dream. Write it down and just like anything else practise, practise, practise.

Go past your goals

Even when you reach your goals you need to keep going.

One of the reasons successful people stop being successful is that they stop when they reach their goals... **they forget to set a new goal.**

You might set a goal to audition and get the role in a play... **success!** If you don't carry on setting more goals, you might just... **fail.**

It feels great to get the part in a play but don't stop there. Your next goal needs to be to learn your lines and give the audience the best show ever.

YOU GET THE IDEA... ONE GOAL IS NOT ENOUGH...

SO WE NEVER GIVE UP.

Don't give up

TRY NEW THINGS

This takes us right back to the beginning of the handbook...

Try lots of new things. This helps us to know:

- **Which things get us in our** E ZONE
- The things we love doing.
- The things we are good at.

When we say never give up that doesn't mean you have to keep doing everything you start. It means never giving up on the things you need to do to be successful.

Successful runners never give up training... **because they need this to be successful...** but they can give up other things like chess.

SECRET SUCCESS SECRET

Know what you need to succeed

Before you say **"Well I don't want to be a scientist so I can give up science?"** just wait a moment. There are usually standards that you have to meet to give you choices. If you don't pass exams when you are older, your choices of what you can do are limited. Most employers need you to meet certain standards in mathematics and English. If you want a career in dance you might be surprised to know that most colleges will also want you to have basic skills in mathematics and English. **That's because you need to be able to communicate whatever you want to do.**

The **rule** is:

'KNOW WHAT YOU NEED TO DO WELL BEFORE YOU GIVE UP ON ANYTHING.'

SUCCESS SECRET

8 Don't give up

HERE ARE THE RULES

Successful people

- ☑ Bounce back from failure.
- ☑ Ignore criticism.
- ☑ Think about success.
- ☑ Try new things.
- ☑ Find out what they need to be successful.

Unsuccessful people

- ☒ Stop when they fail.
- ☒ Get put off by criticism.
- ☒ Don't think about success.
- ☒ Don't try new things.
- ☒ Don't know what they need to be successful.

Which things do you need to do more of so that you don't give up?